THE INTANGIBLE MAN

& OTHER STRANGE TALES

The Intangible Man
& Other Strange Tales
by
Mark Sheeky

Pentangel Books

The Intangible Man
& Other Strange Tales

Written by Mark Sheeky.
Foreword by John F. Keane

With many thanks to Deborah Edgeley for proofreading, technical assistance in
the realm of writing, and for endless support.

Illustrations and graphic design by Mark Sheeky.

1st edition, published by Pentangel Books.
www.pentangel.co.uk
ISBN 978-0-9571947-9-3

To George, wherever he may be

CONTENTS

Foreword by John F. Keane 1

The Irrational Fear of I. B. S. 6
The Incomprehension of Beauty 10
The Door 14
The Puppet Master's Circus 18
The Museum 24
The Geometry of Sleep 32
The Mathematics of Fate 40
The Spider's Web Collector 48
The Text Machine 54
The Voice 62
The Analysis of Joy 68
The Antidote 76
Erasure 82
The Intangible Man 88

Foreword
John F. Keane

I worked with the author of this collection on a collaborative art and poetry exhibition held at Stockport War Memorial Art Gallery in April 2019, and was hugely impressed by his artistic vision and polymathic gifts (he is a composer, novelist, computer programmer, and poet, as well as a visual artist). Despite his many interests, a single vision permeates every activity he undertakes. The nature of this vision is uniquely his own: life-affirming, profoundly visual and aesthetic, drawing inspiration and energy from the vaults of the unconscious, while remaining firmly fixed in the twenty-first century.

When asked to pen an introduction for *The Intangible Man* I jumped at the chance, having enjoyed Mark's excellent novella *The Many Beautiful Worlds of Death* (2015). In sum, *The Intangible Man* is a collection of loosely connected stories exploring the author's interest in the many ways science, philosophy and art intersect with the human condition.

The stories in *The Intangible Man* are a little like those of Jorge Luis Borges – little gnomic parables that leave us questing for their inner meaning. Most of the tales use the same protagonist, a somewhat baffled figure called George whose diffident presence is the only link between the different stories. Even a practical man like me can see that the mystery of artistic creation itself is Sheeky's primary inspiration, 'The Museum', being a good example.

Other stories use traditional science fiction themes like alternative history to explore various topics from the author's novel perspective. 'The Geometry of Sleep' is a good example, where a world in which living things do not sleep is used to explore the nature of dreams and other unconscious mental processes. There are also stories about sentient robots, such as the excellent 'Erasure'. In this gripping piece, a poetic machine contemplates the impending 'reset' of his accreted memories and the loss of 'identity' this will entail. The title story is another scientific parable about the dangers implicit in new and untried technology. Unlike true science fiction, Sheeky's stories never dwell on their technical or scientific contents but rather focus on some psychological, philosophical or moral theme in the manner of Ray Bradbury or Robert Sheckley. However, the surreal juxtapositions and conceptual tangents that define his writing transcend the limitations of genre fiction, frequently achieving that singular vision which defines the highest literature.

Like A. E. Van Vogt or Philip K. Dick, both of whom strove to introduce a new concept every 800 words, Sheeky's hectic style keeps the reader off-balance and intrigued throughout each story. His pacey prose is full of vibrant colour and epic imagery, painting startling word pictures that grip our attention from start to finish. This reminds us that Sheeky is primarily a visual artist and thinks in terms of form, space, and colour far more than most writers. The monochrome illustrations which stud most of these stories explore this visual association, augmenting the vigorous prose while never compromising the reader's imagination.

In conclusion, the reader must prepare to be drained, surprised, entertained, delighted, and amused by the *The Intangible Man*.

STRANGE TALES

The Irrational Fear
of Irritable Bowel Syndrome

George's gaunt face peered through the thick, warm, Victorian glass of the junk shop window. The display was cluttered with dusty objects of brass and ivory, small paintings with ornate frames, and steely parts of rusted mechanisms. His eyes were transfixed by a pocket watch which was hanging loose from the hands of an elephant-god. The watch was swinging, almost imperceptibly, left and right, its fine chain trembling as the warm links cut through the air of the dark shop's interior.

He stepped in from the grey winter's morning. The top of the green door kissed a small bell as he entered. The room was crammed to the ceiling with objects, and the air between smelled of yellowed books. A winding passage cut through the maze of junk. There was no shopkeeper in sight. George was pleased to browse alone and avoid the feelings of suspicious awkwardness that a lone customer and lone shopkeeper exchange.

The room began to quake. Slowly at first, then growing in intensity, clattering china saucer against cup, and causing stacks of wooden furniture to shudder so that they made a noise like beetles' wings in excited flurry. A train was passing, alerting George to the underground railway beneath his feet. Soon the shop relaxed into its dim peace. The watch in the window twisted and rocked.

'H-hello?' said George, peering nervously towards the empty sales desk.

Silence.

'Hello?' he said with more conviction.

No reply.

There was a small room behind the desk, visible through an opening flanked by stacks of cardboard boxes, one of which was leaking typewriters. The room was lit by a yellow light. He moved closer and carefully stepped in. A bare bulb hung from the ceiling, with a fez above it as a shade. There was a mug of steaming tea on a brown curved desk strewn with papers. A cake; soft, warm, and rich sat dolloped on a plate. It was crawling with caterpillars. A train passed making the room shudder. The fez gently swayed left then right, casting shadows like the horizon seen from a storm-set galleon.

A loud clang noise sounded; a grandfather clock began the chime of four. George quickly decided to leave and headed for the door. Beyond the glass, which seemed of infinite thickness, was infinite blackness. The door was sealed. A feint, rapid ticker-tap signalled the start of another passing train and the room began to shudder and shake. Some books from a high shelf shivered and dived to the floor far below with a terminal slap.

George noticed a large stuffed owl to his left at the far end of the shop. The owl's head slowly rotated to face him. The owl's expression was frozen in terror. A tear-drop leaked from the corner of its living, human eye; the eyes were George's. The sound of the quaking shop was deafening. The owl's abdomen burst in an explosion of fluff.

The Incomprehension of Beauty

George looked at the pocket watch in his left hand. It had a large gold case with curling scrolls that ran about the surface in elegant baroque. He clicked it open with his thumb and looked at the pearl face. The time was a quarter to two.

The sky was overcast, a smooth cream of white, and the crisp breeze of the morning made the fallen leaves dance in a clattering roll along the pavement. George was standing in front of the jewellers, the shop from where his wife, Julia, had bought the watch before she died. George already had a reliable digital watch and he couldn't understand why she had given him this expensive and unnecessary gift. He had decided to return it to the shop.

He went in through the revolving doors and tapped along the marble floor. There were no other customers present, and a thin shop assistant with circular spectacles soon appeared and enquired: 'Can I help you sir?'

'My wife bought this watch here a few days ago. I'd like to return it. Here.'

He handed the watch over.

The man looked at it with confusion: 'We don't...' he began. 'We...'

The bespectacled man was transfixed by the watch. He turned it over, and with a squeeze he opened the back of the case to peer at the workings. A tiny regular rapping noise, like the exhale of a dozen praying beetles, was heard. All else was silent and still.

'We...' said the man, in near whisper. His eyes were locked upon the inner parts of the device. He closed the lid with a neat click and handed the watch back. 'I don't understand it.' he said firmly. 'This is not ours. I cannot accept it. Good day to you, sir.'

The street had fewer people now. The wide road, empty, steel-grey, flowed from left to right like a cold mechanical river. George moved across, eyes on the opposite shore. A horn screamed at him from his left, he turned, startled. Something big and heavy slammed into his left side and his body was kicked into the sky. His arms flailed, a doll falling. A woman screamed. His body crunched and folded into the concrete floor. Blackness.

A greenish light filled the operating theatre. George lay unconscious on the table. A steel blade cut into him exposing his insides. Gold parts ticked and turned. There were fine rubies at the centre of each rotating wheel, and in the middle of his chest a coil expanding and contracting with a regular pulse and flow. 'We can do nothing here.' said the surgeon.

George awoke in an empty ward. He sat up, each tiny movement marked by laser agonies that shot from his right shoulder and cut through the centre of his damaged body. He swallowed. By his bedside on a small table he saw the watch. He took it in his right hand. He opened the back and a tiny white dove flew out in a ray of golden light. In perfect symmetry it ascended before vanishing quickly. George tilted the watch towards him and looked inside.

In the back of the watch was a scene of paradise, a lush globe of garden. In the perfect light-blue sky were the gold mechanical parts of the watch, slowly turning and marking time. The ground was summer grass, a meadow of warm, soft-scented beauty. Birds circled distant mountain peaks, tinged with cool snow, around which the flows of air smelt of the purest oxygen. A lake of smooth, clear water was visible, and on its shore was a metal framed hospital bed. George could see himself in the bed.

Suddenly a bell rang, and the beds in the ward were full of patients and the hum of chatter. The double doors at the end of the room opened and visitors flowed in. A man came in who looked like George, exactly like George. The man looked around and headed for the bed.

George pushed his broken body up in his bed, and was stabbed by a micro-agony. The watch in his right hand felt heavy and comforting. He looked at it, and saw that his hand was now female, his arm thin and hairless. Both hands were female, his body too. He was female. He had become Julia, George's wife.

The visitor stepped over to her bed. Julia looked at him with eyes of peace and love. She swallowed and handed him the watch and said: 'This is for you.'

The Door

It was an external house door, brick red, in a tough, shiny, enamel paint. There was a brass knob enrobed with snakes of metal, and its baseplate possessed an alluring keyhole. Four panels divided up the surface. The door had appeared in the middle of the north-facing wall of the front room during the night. It was sealed tight.

George stared at this new visitor with a curious eagerness. He remembered that he had seen it before, in a catalogue he had fleetingly observed in the garden centre a few days earlier. That day was tedious trawl among the lonely plants, a day beset and defined by a grey listlessness which the trip with June had not coloured.

Now here was the door in glorious redness; magically present, like a secret wish made manifest. He wanted to open it but didn't know if he should. He called to June and she walked in, arms animated in preparation to leave for work. She looked at the door with unimpressed eyes and sent George a disapproving glance.

'Right, I'm leaving,' she said, leaning towards George to accept a forthcoming kiss on the cheek.

'See you.'

She left the house briskly and floated out of sight.

George put his face close to the door, breathing in the skin of oxygen that flowed across its surface. He looked down and brushed the cold brass with the limp fingers of his right hand. He had to know what was beyond. He grabbed the knob firmly, turning it until the bolt was fully withdrawn and pulled on the door. It was locked.

He bent down and peered at the lock with a cocked right eye, then furtively dashed outside to the garage to fetch his biggest screwdriver, the one that had never seen a screw in its long life, its perfect engineering instead being used for manual jobs like opening recalcitrant tins of paint, mock-chiselling, and that sort of thing. George returned and stabbed it into the crevice near the lock, forcing it sideways and crunching the fresh wood into tiny splinters. He stepped back and looked at the damaged paintwork for a few guilty seconds. This was hopeless, a key was needed. The locksmith on the high street would provide one cheaply in exchange for a believable story. George grabbed his coat and left the house, mentally rehearsing and refining the exact words he would say.

In the end, the key was obtained quite easily, the locksmith seeming to feel quite sorry for the man. The key's surface was highly polished gold. It produced a polite tone in collision with the front door key as he let himself back in. George went into the front room. The door now had three planks of wood nailed across it, making a crude ladder shape. George went to the garage and returned with a claw hammer and began to remove the planks, wrenching each one from the wall with fervour. Each nail gave a crisping, forlorn cry as the iron hammer bit into the soft planks.

The door was now exposed. He inserted the key, and turned the lock which clicked with a wondrous delight. He turned the knob, and pulled the door open with fervour and nervous excitement.

The door opened to a spring meadow of lush grass. Young wild flowers nodded their heads in chime to fresh breezes, which meandered through a verdant paradise. He saw an apple tree courted by a bird, something like a hummingbird or kingfisher, a creature of dazzling beauty. Its slender beak of gold reflected the young, yellow sun, which shone from some distant point behind the newly opened portal.

George's gaze was fixed upon the bird when it turned and suddenly fell from flight, dead. Brown clouds rolled at hurricane speed, and an immense and terrifying quake of thunder sent waves of booming sound through George's chest. A shock of brilliant lightning smashed the tree, and the lush meadow began to decay. Like a domino-topple from the door, a wave of brown death flowed in ripples. Plants curled up in seconds, stiffened, and crumbled to dust as though burned by an invisible ray. Soon, the most distant blue peaks had become grey and volcanic. A distant flying creature fell in black spiral like a lost umbrella. The scene of paradise had become a dry wasteland of barren soil. This terrible malady stemmed from the door. George knew that he had caused this. An immense feeling of guilt and horror fell upon him.

June was now in the room, weeping profusely, huddled alone on the sofa like a frightened mouse. She looked up at George with pink eyes of agony and hatred. George began to panic and grabbed at the edge of the smooth, painted door for reassurance.

A stocky man in a dark, pin-stripe suit walked into the room and moved past George with brash efficiency. He firmly closed the door and locked it with his own key, then produced a black pistol and shot George three times in the face.

The Puppet Master's Circus

It was lunch time and George pushed open the heavy glass doors of the museum, and stepped in from the sunlight. The familiar sight of the foyer, enrobed in greens and brassy brown marble, greeted his relieved eyes as he made his way up the vast, curling staircase, past the ornate columns, and entered gallery number twelve to sit in his usual seat.

He carefully unpacked his sandwiches, and stared at the painting once more. The Puppet Master's Circus, painted nearly forty years ago, looked as fresh and exciting now as it had the first time he saw it. The masterpiece was filled with elaborate detail, hundreds of people, monsters, and fine objects in the style of classical antiquity.

George was there for a specific reason today; a specific and fantastical reason that few would believe. A few days ago he was sure he noticed a new figure in the painting, a new dancer that was not there a week ago. Yesterday he had carefully scrutinised the painting, and today he was amazed to confirm the appearance of two more people. At the same time, the gallery seemed to be growing increasingly empty.

He noticed a pretty young woman seated on the next bench, her eyes transfixed, with a gaze of awe and puzzlement, upon the painting. She blinked slowly.

'It's an amazing picture isn't it?' said George nervously.

'Yes...' she replied, in distant thought. 'You know... I'm sure that there are more people in it than I remember.'

'So you've noticed it too! That dancer, the one dressed like a harlequin. He wasn't there yesterday.'

'There's something about it...' said the woman, still distant.

A loud bell, like a fire bell, rang for a short stab, sending reverberations throughout the cold halls of the gallery. The woman awoke from her trance and looked at George. 'I'm Samantha.' she said, extending a delicate hand. 'Pleased to meet you.'

'George. Sorry, I must dash. It's my lunch hour and I have to return to work. It was nice to meet you. I often come here for lunch. Perhaps I'll see you again..?'

'Perhaps.' said Samantha with a quick smile.

George flashed a smile back and hurried from the building. Down the staircase, past the iron clock in the foyer, out, and back to the dark office and drab job that had defined his life for as long as he could remember. At least that afternoon he would have the warm glow of a new friend for company.

George changed his lunch routine on the next day, diverting into the public library. The great hall smelt of damp wallpaper, the familiar musty yellowness that pervades each truly old building. The book shelves were dark, polished wood, and meticulously kept by the attentive long-nosed librarian, and his neatly dressed staff. The French-polished tables in the research area were equally elegant, and George sat at one, his face soon lit by the glow from the computer terminal as he sought the address of the artist, the painter of The Puppet Master's Circus. His name was Samuel Preeter, and as George was aware, he was still living somewhere in London. George located the address and scribbled it down with a stubby pencil. He glanced at his wristwatch. It was nearly time to visit the gallery. He briskly stood and left.

The museum was even more quiet than usual today. In the vault of the main entrance hall the streaming sunlight made square patterns of light, fringed with rainbow colours. He dashed up the wide staircase and into his gallery. He really wanted Samantha to be there, but he was disappointed. In fact the room was empty. He exhaled an inaudible sigh and extracted his last sandwich from the wrapping, ambling around the quiet room.

He was halfway through a bite when he saw her. Her face peeking out, just to the right of the laughing juggler. Her eyes as fascinated as they were yesterday. Red coat, and short blonde curls. Barely visible, just a tiny scrap of face among the tumult of people and wide fingered ferns. Samantha was in the painting, painted with lucid clarity; complementing the composition as though she had always been there.

The bell rang, waking George from his hypnotic slumber. For a microsecond he thought about going to see the artist, right there and then, but an insecurity gripped him and he felt compelled to stick to his routine. He would return to work as normal and go to see the artist tomorrow morning.

The walk to the home of Mr. Preeter was like taking a trip back in time. The busy streets of central London gave way to quieter, twisted alleys. Parked cars became heavy framed black bicycles, and the accents of the street people became Victorian caricatures, as George weaved and swam through the stone columns and street entertainers of the capital.

He arrived at the house shortly before twelve o'clock. The town house had a heavy front door, shiny and navy blue, with brass adornments in the middle. He rang the bell and waited.

Mr. Preeter open the door with a welcoming smile. He wore a fez and pince-nez, and greying sideburns at least a century out of fashion. He was wearing what looked like workman's overalls and Wellington boots, portraying quite the most eccentric fellow that George had ever seen. 'Come in! Come in!' Preeter said, seeming to recognise George. He gestured skywards with the poetic flurry of a romantic composer, then immediately turned away, heading for the dark chambers of the residence.

'Umm..?' said George loudly, a little confused, but he was ignored by the artist who was already striding away. George followed at a trot, closing the front door behind him.

'This way. This way!' boomed Preeter 'You know the way!'

Mr. Preeter sank through a dark opening to the right and George hurried to catch him.

There was no sign of the artist in the chamber. It was octagonal, and festooned with marble. Eight grooved columns supported a circular domed ceiling clad with regular square panels. Four petal-shaped windows near the apex of the dome showed distant clouds gently passing by. Two long-leaved plants from a desert country bowed their foliage gracefully towards the exit opening. The room was quite beautiful, and exactly matched the mood and texture of the painting that so fascinated George.

Preeter was nowhere to be seen or heard. George felt quite alone, yet the clean white angles of this room instantly made him feel at peace. On the wall to the right was a striking velvet curtain of a shimmering crimson hue, covering something on the wall. A gold braided cord hung tantalisingly beside it. George so wanted to see what was behind the curtain. What could it be? Some great unseen masterpiece... or the eternally covered portrait of a lost love..?

He pulled the cord and the curtain slid open revealing a window with a gilt frame.

George was stunned. The window looked out into gallery number twelve, the room he visited each day and knew so well. He could see familiar paintings on the distant wall, and right in front of the opening he could see his bench. Samantha stepped into view, staring straight in at the window, scrutinizing the space with fascination, apparently oblivious to George's presence.

In the gallery, Samantha looked at the portrait with curious eyes. It was executed with flair and brilliance, but how strange the subject. The painting showed a man, sitting in a sumptuous Roman palace eating a limp cheese sandwich made with white bread. The man looked like George. 'Excuse me?' She enquired, to a curiously dressed man who was facing away 'Do you know anything about this painting?'

The man turned. He was a somewhat strange and eccentric fellow named Samuel J. Preeter. 'Yes!' he exclaimed with enthusiasm 'I know this! It looks so modern doesn't it? - but, you know, this was painted over a century ago. It's called The Puppet Master's Circus.'

The Museum

'It is here. It is here somewhere...'

His torch beam flicked from glass case to case, casting its viscous glow through the thick panes of the green, iron glass. He peered intensely at the exhibits inside. It was night at the museum and George was the only thing moving. He had been searching for some time.

In the upper corner of the chamber, the tiny red dot of a security camera betrayed the presence of a hidden eye. The lens gently rotated to adjust focus.

George moved closer to a large case in the middle of the room. It was wide and flat, like a glass coffin, and low enough for him to lean right over it and look at its contents from above. The olive floor tiles ran up to its sloping edge like a dead plain touching a rectangular mountain. Directly overhead, in the ceiling, was an angular window, edged with white-painted wrought iron. The moon beamed in a thin light from an empty sky beyond.

He bent down low and touched the side of the case with his eager fingers, peering intensely at the rags inside. He squinted and illuminated the object, a mummy clad in desiccated brown shreds. George's breath misted the glass. He stood up tall and craned his neck to get an overhead look.

'Maybe...' he whispered.

The camera stared at him.

The museum was vast. It was built an age ago and made of thick, cold stone that made every sound echo. The marble tiled rooms were lined with heavy brass radiators, and wood and glass cabinets. The main entrance was a wide, sweeping, semi-circular chamber in green stone and rich mahogany browns. Two smooth columns, too wide to embrace, stretched to a high domed ceiling and flanked two swinging doors of polished walnut and elaborately patterned stained glass. The entrance hall was the cleanest and neatest place in the building. It was most important that it should be so. Deeply etched words ran around the base of dome. Words draped in unmoving shadow.

The swinging doors led to the history room, displaying the crisp, parchment writings of great minds, old posters and toys in dioramas, and creepy glass tanks, rocks and fossils of the world, pickled animals in gloomy liquids in wide necked jars, seed cases, dead beetles and pinned butterflies in drawer after drawer after drawer, brass handles polished, the front neatly labelled in a fine violet script.

The unpleasant smell of formaldehyde oozed from the gaps in the cabinet, flowing over and along the floor towards the open exit in the north wall; a Gothic Revival arch of Victorian blocks that led to a long gallery, lined on both sides with paintings of men in dark suits beside wives with blue dresses and unsmiling eyes. There was a picture of naked maidens laughing by a river. A very dark miniature of a beautiful face painted with perfect care. Dusty fruit with flies. The hall ended with two uninspiring abstracts, the last a brown and green comment made in nineteen-eighteen. A comment that beauty was asleep.

A heavy square door at the end swung into an octagonal, white-marble chamber of classical sculpture, which then branched off into different wings. To the east, the circular music room displayed period musical instruments on a plush crimson carpet. There were four instruments, all capable of playing; a harp with a vertical in the form of the goddess Venus, a cello in rich varnished wood, a lovely silver flute under a heavy glass cloche, and a harpsichord in black lacquer, with a country scene painted on the lid. All of the instruments were enveloped in a layer of dust, apart, that is, from the flute, protected forever underneath its transparent shell.

Years before, as a young man, George would play these instruments in his secret forays into the empty building. He was well acquainted with how to get in and out. By now he had worked out that nobody would hear him no matter how loudly he played.

His first break-in was thrilling. He had crept into the building though a small square window near the floor, using a piece of bent wire poked through the narrow gap to lift the latch. It didn't look like the window had been touched in years, certainly not cleaned, it was misted with a curious circular patten, as though a spectral grey ball had casually floated through the middle of it one day. The window was near the top of a dark storage room, a room piled with damp smelling boxes of old records, straggles of tape, and yellowed music manuscripts. Of all of the things there, George most noted a frame on the wall containing a black and white photograph of a pop star whom his parents adored. The man in the picture was dark suited, wearing sunglasses, slightly to the side and smiling, shaking hands with an old man as both were snapped by the eager flashbulbs of the local newspaper photographers. George kept that room in order, and left the window just open enough to make his future entrances and exits easier.

By contrast to the awkwardness of entering the museum on that night, he found playing the harpsichord joyously easy. He had no experience of playing a musical instrument, and was amazed at the discovery that it was as simple as pressing the right keys. In the years since that time he had become a good player of each instrument, and a good composer too. This said, he hadn't yet tried the flute. The glass dome would not be easy to safely remove, and he feared that his fingerprints would betray his presence.

During each performance his playing was observed by the music room camera near the ceiling. In some ways it was sad that the cameras didn't record sound.

Now though, the instruments were silent, and the room was sitting empty in near darkness. A journey from the golden tip of the harp, over the lacquer harpsichord, wheeling back out of the room, west through the sculpture room, and onwards, led to a cubic chamber lined with objects macabre and fascinating. A shrunken head, a comb made from human bone, pointed objects wrested from the weak hands of old Australian aborigines, the terrifying mask of a Samurai warrior.

The middle area of this room contained large, floor-standing cases, and George was now peering into one. This area was 'Anthropology'.

He was moving excitedly now. The case was heavy. How did it open?! He grabbed the glass firmly, leaning over and gripping both sides. He pulled but couldn't move the box. He paused and stared again at the mummy, then inhaled. He glanced left and right, he needed something to smash the glass with. The torch. Yes! He made a tight fist around the light and smashed it down confidently. The heavy glass broke into four huge pieces with a tremendous cracking sound.

The red light on the camera blinked. The camera in the picture gallery stared at the face of the beautiful miniature, catching a pink arm from a naked maiden from the picture next to it, the whole scene lit by the smooth, blue beams of the cool moon.

The echo resounded throughout the building. In the history

room, a moth's wings moved, ever so slightly, as if inspired by a recollection of a warm wind.

The moth was once a tiny thread of yellow-green, sniffing the air on minute black dots of legs, making delicate arcs on a crisp, furry leaf in a faraway country. A warm, saline breeze spiralled around the plantation, beneath an orange tropical sun that shone waves of summer music and childhood memories. Each crisping lettuce bite by the tiny jaws was a notch, marked like the rings in a tree, or like the curling groove on a record, a molecule of memory, set and recorded inside the caterpillar for long term storage. Some time later, the damp new moth emerged from its cocoon, spreading new and perfect wings, patterned with black lines on golden browns, like the roads of a map, like the branching paths in a brain carved through the crunching, matted nets of cells when young, then trodden more easily as thoughts flowed like water down familiar routes.

Now the streams were dry. The pattern fixed. The moth captured and protected underneath a silent ceiling of glass, and a mist of formaldehyde. Neatly labelled, in case any eye should ever read it.

The sculpture room had a brown stone floor of intricate swirling patterns. Where the flat walls joined there were vertical rails made of gilded plaster with Rococo embellishments. The ceiling was domed in glass, segmented by metal ribs, and suspended from the centre was a vast chandelier made of silver with a storm of crystal droplets. It was most beautiful on sunny days when the room was filled with voices. A host of tiny rainbows would dance in the breeze like butterflies.

George loved to look that chandelier. It was the thing he most remembered from his first visit as a small boy. His mother made him go inside on his own one day when she had to visit the hospital. He was scared at first, but soon began to love his trips to the museum.

His mother was blind, yet confident. Used to relying on other people, she wanted to make sure that her son was as independent as possible, often giving him the tasks and responsibilities of a much older child. George couldn't always manage them, but he learned, and was eager to please his mother. In fact, she seemed rather unpleasable. No matter what George did, he seemed to need to do more to receive some affection. This had the effect of feeding his imagination and desire to learn. He read as much as he could as a child, and as a young man was fixed on the idea of becoming an artist. When he worked at the museum he had a special room at the back, behind a green wooden door for 'authorised personnel only'. It was there that he painted, and wrote the labels for his collection in a fine violet script.

But now George was older, and the labels had decayed from white to cream. His current obsession was the body in front of him, lying in the shattered case that he had arranged there so long ago that he had forgotten how or when. He removed his right glove with his teeth and urgently pulled off the left one, at all times fixed on the face of the mummy. Trying his best to be careful, he eagerly pulled away the rotted bandages. Slowly unwinding the wraps from the heavy head. He was trembling with excitement. A shock of flesh appeared, a first glimpse of forehead. He continued.

From a high corner behind him, the hollow electric eye of the camera gazed at the ever active figure. Along its sleek black wire, the signals were pushed into the dark control room, the sealed box in the depths of the museum with a wall of television screens that showed every room in black and white, from every angle: the heavy brass and glass door at the entrance; the history room piled with towers of paper, old photographs, ornaments, scents, dead insects; the moonlit picture gallery; the white marble sculpture room; the silent music room; anthropology.

The images were not recorded. There was nobody in the security room. There had never been anybody in the security room; and the only person ever seen shuffling on the screens was the solitary occupant, the man who had built the museum and created everything inside.

The Geometry of Sleep

The noise from the protesters outside sounded like the night rain, humming and hissing, the sound pulsing like the heavy drips in the white, conical beams of the street-lights high above. The thick window shielded the staff inside, muting the hubbub of the stalwart crowd beyond. An avenue of police, wearing yellow jackets, flanked the sweeping main entrance to the new building. Red-brick floor, weedless. A building of blue steel and black gold glass, that looked sleek and modern in the architect's office, and forbidding and mysterious in the bleak November rain of central London.

Beyond the glass Doctor Mentis sat by George's bed, perched on the tip of a white, iron-framed chair. His hands were clasped, twisting together like an anxious clam. George looked dead, his eyes closed, yet his eyeballs were moving beneath their lids, darting left and right. The doctor pulled a left knuckle to his lips, and looked at the array of silver needles on the machine. The machine was connected by a spiral of wires, and neat tape, to George's shaved head. The needles ticked left and right, scribbling their secret brain code onto a long roll of paper that slopped onto the floor.

A woman's voice pulled the doctor from his thoughts: 'Is it time to administer the antidote?'

Doctor Mentis drew some fingers across his lips slowly. 'Not yet. Let's see if he will awaken normally.'

There was a bang at the huge window; a dull thud, as the bulky frame of a bearded, leather-clad man fell against it. The doctor stood, making his chair groan on the hard floor. 'An accident,' said the female researcher. The man outside was on the floor, arms grasping. His placard on its thin white pole tumbled in the rain. The words 'SLEEP IS GOD'S DOMAIN' flashed at the doctor as the sign twisted and fell. Some people lifted the man to his feet.

The doctor wrung his hands again and sat back down, his eyes on the restful face of George. George was the first person to experience sleep. Not the first creature; that was Emelda, a small, white, cloned mouse, who, on June the eleventh had been administered the first ever dose of a new drug, Hypnorin-1414. The drug rendered the mouse unconscious, and a few hours later the mouse awoke. Emelda was the first known creature to sleep, an event that made her world famous. Her achievement was headline news across the globe.

Until that point the scientific community was divided on the subject of sleep. Some thought it was impossible, a state of living death from which nobody could recover. There had been cases of comatose patients, people with traumatic brain injuries spontaneously regaining consciousness, but their memories were too damaged to recall anything useful about their experience. Under a microscope cells seemed to experience regular dormant periods. It seemed as though life was capable of a unique state between life and death, the 'sleep' that was engrained in religious mythology. Up to half of the population believed that life could exist inside sleep, a second life, a new domain shared by other sleepers. Some believed that sleep was a gateway to another universe, a dangerous gateway. But it was all speculation. Nobody had slept. Not ever. Few wanted to. The concept was alien, feared. The dead slept, and they did not awaken.

Yet, about one hundred metres away, wheeling along a hard grey corridor lit with buzzing yellow-green tube lights, through a heavy, fire-proof, coded orange door, inside a wire cage populated by clean wood shavings and a blue plastic food bowl, was the huddled ball of a small white mouse that had known sleep. In the wall behind, a larger rectangular cage that rattled and rung when touched, was a small rhesus monkey that had also slept. While asleep, the monkey's eyes had moved, and its brain had showed a remarkably high level of activity. This information had been suppressed by the researchers, but Adric Richter had forced the publication of this publicly funded research.

Outside, now, in the tarmac clad car-park of this building, standing in the silver shards of 3am rain was Adric Richter. In his black, woollen coat, a huge silver revolver was hanging in its holster. Six shots were loaded, shielded from the downpour and the muffled regular chants of the large gathering at the entrance, fifty or so metres ahead. Adric pulled his coat around his neck and lowered the tip of the distinctive brown fedora he liked to wear. A stream of rain-water ran from the brim and cascaded past his face, tumbling away towards a unseen stream below.

The green river was wide here and ran for one hundred and seventy miles from this point. It was dusk in the jungle, viscous and fragrant like a wax factory. Dayton Richter, Adric's father, was in a wooden hospital. Under a mosquito net in a flimsy bed was a young Adric, feverish. Adric could see people and hear voices, sounds blurred as though underwater. He was too hot, uncomfortable. His head hurt. The flickering light from the lantern made his eyes sting. There was a breeze from his left, and the net curtain pulsed a single romantic curl. Beyond it something moved, in the shadow, near the bed opposite. An animal. A cat. It was a huge black cat. The cat lifted a paw, pulling its pendulous digits together, then placed them slowly down, splayed flat. Its head was locked in space, hovering, staring at his prey: Adric. The boy drew in a stuttering breath. The cat's eyes were like yellow diamonds. The pupils suddenly shot wide, ready to pounce. 'N-no!' cried Adric. He held up an arm, he tried to, it was trapped beneath his covers. He screamed in terror, 'No!'

'He's delirious.' said an African voice.

His father touched his burning head and placed a damp cloth on it. 'Shhh, now just rest,' he said quietly.

In the research room the needles of the machine began to carve a wide circle, and then, as one, level out. George slowly opened his eyes and took a deep breath.

'Subject is awake,' said the doctor. He twisted his wrist and glanced at the slim hands of his Swiss watch, 'at three eleven and four seconds.'

George crunched some fingers into his brow and pulled himself into a sitting position, dragging a hissing trail of fine wire curls across the back of his white metal bed. It was a curious feeling, to be in bed. George hadn't been in a bed before. It was a piece of furniture associated with the elderly or the sick. He smoothed the surface of the covers with his right hand.

There was a bright flash of lightning outside, beyond the wide black window. The doctors looked up. A second flash. A man's face was illuminated. A man in a long dark outfit and wearing a hat with a wide brim. The man withdrew his arm from the inner folds of his coat, his grip tight on the handle of a large revolver. He slowly focused the gun on the doctor, the man lit up brightly and seated next to the bed, just three or four metres from the mouth of the silver weapon. The startled target stood up, his arms frozen in mid air as if held by invisible puppet strings. Eyes wide.

Adric pulled the trigger and a blast of yellow fire shot from the barrel of the gun. The metal slug swam through the thick,

November air, then slammed through the plate glass, cracking the vast window into huge pieces that screamed loudly as they twisted and fell to the brick floor. With a smooth flow, a beam of smoke drew a keen line from the pistol through the chest of the stunned doctor, cutting the sterile laboratory air and crunching a good way into the powdery plaster of the opposite wall.

George sat up and turned, shuffling in the bed and ripping away the coils of wire. The doctor was lying dead, flopped backwards like a rolled up rug. His glasses slid off his face and clattered to the ground. George grabbed a handful of covers and pulled them away frantically, managing to clear enough space for a leg, which he duly placed on the floor. A smell like smoke and rain hit his nostrils. A dark man was in the room with him. The man raised his gun and pointed it at George.

'This is a door,' the man said.

The killer's finger tightened on the nickel trigger, heaving back the hammer like an archer pulling a bowstring. Soundless and smoothly, the hammer reached its apex, and then fell forwards, head first like a charging rhinoceros towards the brassy percussion cap that smashed a ring of cordite in a star-spray. There was a crack sound, and from the tip of the gun something white appeared. White and slow. Tumbling through space, head over feet. It was a mouse, a tiny white mouse. Time was pulled like toffee, and George stared at the mouse in the air, its tiny, pink eyes appeared shocked, then more relaxed, as the mouse began to change shape. The furry creature stretched itself into stability, and then grew longer. Wings appeared, like tiny nodules on the shoulders at first, then larger and wider. The pointed nose became a hard beak, and the long tail fanned out into an array of white feathers. The mouse had become a dove. It reared up, fluttering and rattling, and then turned its head towards the shattered window. Beyond it, dawn was breaking, and beams of yellow sun were shining through into the lab. The bird flew out of the window, and high, to freedom beyond. George felt wonderful.

He opened his eyes. He was lying in bed. It was daylight. Doctor Mentis was there, looking at him with a gentle smile.

'What was it like?' he asked.

The Mathematics of Fate

A man with ripples of gold hair, wearing polished bronze armour, and on horseback; a beautiful grey white dappled horse of immense strength. The man turned with a smile and extended an arm to hold a short sword high, a signal. There were others here; soldiers of some sort, from an ancient time, some on horseback too, and others on foot carrying huge lances with sharp tips.

The silver blade of the sword reflected a shock of sunlight at George, who flashed a flurry of blinks, then shielded his delicate eyes with one hand. The blond man uttered a cry in a strange language and rode away. The sky behind him was a vivid beautiful blue, warm, like a high summer in Alpine mountains. George noticed one cloud. It looked like a skull.

'Alexander the Great.' George whispered to himself. 'Died aged...'

The scene faded into whiteness. George put down his smart silver engineers' pen and placed his fingertips together, touching them to his lips. The familiar hum of the people returned, a gentle babble, like a liquid train flowing over the tracks of the bingo hall. This room was rectangular, and had a squeaky polished floor of new, light wood. The high ceiling was gridded with an array of tan tiles, separated by small metal strips that shot across it like robotic roads. Florescent tube lights, topped with angular iron shades, hung from metal chains making them swing gently as though moved by the thoughts of the players below. The room was moderately full on that rainy Thursday night, about fifty people were there. It was used for bingo each week, and George had been coming to play for just over a year.

'Buckle my shoe. Thirty two!' smiled Keith down the microphone. He popped the yellow ball onto the wooden rack on the stage. About half of the balls had been drawn so far. Someone would probably win soon.

George flashed a smile. He crossed through thirty-two on his card. Two more numbers left. Just two. The prize tonight was ten thousand pounds. It wasn't easy to win; you had to accumulate several games. It had taken George eight weeks to get this far.

He looked down at his card with a keen focus. 'Sixty six next,' he whispered.

George was thirty-seven years old. He had been living alone since leaving university where he studied mathematics, first calculus then specialising in topology. For his Ph. D thesis he wrote a paper on multi-dimensional folding that helped Dr. Abrams Spillane win the Nobel Prize for Physics six years earlier. George felt that he should have shared the prize. Dr. Spillane acknowledged the importance of George's paper. George even appealed to the Nobel committee, but Spillane didn't share the prize. Not the money. George's second academic paper was about the application of probability in multiple universes. It was a quite brilliant work. There was an equation at the end, something incredible and simple and beautiful that nobody had seen or considered before. And nobody had seen it since, either. George had decided not to publish the paper.

He placed his marker down carefully to the right of his card, then punched some numbers into the sleek, black scientific calculator that lay askance, next to the garish pink bingo card. He glanced up ahead, to the wide, moon face of the circular clock on the opposite wall. A sweeping second hand was running up along the surface. The bingo machine on the stage was fizzing and bubbling, churning the brightly coloured bingo balls like an eager paint mixer. A number would be chosen soon. Time was short.

George picked up his engineers' pen and tore a new page on the plain white notepad below the calculator. He wrote something hurriedly in dark blue ink. It was a calculation, a formula, rapidly scratched and scribbled, the symbols slurred with the energy and genius of the writer. Before him, the lines began to move, like sand in a shifting desert. Straight lines began to bend and sway like summer wheat. The shapes curled and swirled, forming a picture, a moving image. A connection was being made, a bridge between two worlds. George stared at the page and began to see faces and hear music.

It was dark at first, very dim. He was inside a room with walls of coarse brick, no, more like cobbled stones, of a greenish-grey that shone as though polished. There were people around, five or six, perhaps more. There was a bright white light, a small spotlight in a black metal case, hanging from a horizontal rail that ran from one side of the room to the other. There was a second light to the left, and a glitterball that was gently revolving to and fro, like a dancing planet. A stream of smoke touched his nostrils and the chatter of the people increased in volume and clarity. It was English. Scouse. This was somewhere in Liverpool, then. A drum started and George noticed that the lights were part of a stage. A drumbeat, then a droning hum. A tone like a running river, swirling and curling along a line of sound. The rhythm was pounding, hypnotic. More lights appeared, in pinks and vivid purples, flashing and glowing in phases in time to the music, music that played and howled like the ribbon of sound that flowed from a snake charmers flute. A singer stepped up to a microphone on a silver spear of a stand. It was John Lennon's voice. It was John. It was the Beatles. The song was Tomorrow Never Knows.

'This must be nineteen...'

'Clickety click, sixty six,' said Keith down the microphone.

George crossed through his equation and ripped off the page. One number left. He grabbed the bingo marker and sliced through sixty six. The number eighty-five remained. Just eighty-five. One number.

Outside, the rain tumbled earthwards in gulps. A flash of lightning lit up the white, breeze-block walls of the building. A deep rumble permeated the air, causing the lights to shudder on their chains. A few fragments of dust, and flecks of paint from the ceiling, fell on George's desk. He brushed them aside with a few swift motions of his hand. He was holding his silver pen; hexagonal aluminium, a neat and efficient writing instrument. A graduation present from his grey-haired architect father.

He clicked off the calculator and slid the white notepad closer, rapidly scribbling the next equation. On the stage the bingo machine was turning and boiling, juggling the myriad numbered balls. Somewhere inside that transparent plastic cauldron was a light blue ball, bashed and knocked. Diving, running, swimming among the others. A light blue ball inscribed eighty-five. A light blue ball worth ten thousand pounds.

George cast a furtive sideways glance at the stage. Keith Mermonshet was beaming in his sparkly suit, gripping the black and blue microphone, and staring at the ever active machine. On the wall, the thin black hand on the white disc face of the clock was slicing another minute away.

George had finished. He dropped the pen. On the page, the lines began to shift and turn. Seeking a path, a route to the number eighty-five. That was the key. The important thing. The equations demanded a target, and the target was a number. Across time and space the mathematics stretched like a mystical rubber-band. Searching, probing, testing. Unlocking.

Outside, the sky raged and boiled, cycling like a tornado, forming fingers of cloud and holes, tunnels that reached to the stars and beyond to touch distant space. Torrents of rain cascaded down like toys thrown at the earth by the gods. The water smashed onto the roof of the bingo hall. In the air above, something was forming, a spark of something magical, something connected to the white page below and the stars above. Something hot and energetic, pulling from all directions like a greedy child: a ball of white power. It exploded into life, a sphere of lightning, hot as a blue sun. Down it flew, darting left and right like a racing swift, in zigs and zags towards the ground, then; slam! The finger of energy hit the ribbed metal roof of the bingo hall, melting into the skin of the building and still running through its bones like a gaggle of electric rats, targeting a chain, a chain in a ceiling, a chain above George that was gently quivering, waiting for fate to arrive.

George was staring at the white page. Something felt wrong. He saw tumbling clouds of black and purple; darkness. There was a flash in the ceiling above and a shower of sparks, like a waterfall of fire, fell about him. A woman screamed. One of the chains had broken and the light was falling, swinging on the remaining chain. George looked up, startled. Like an axe, the heavy, angular metal swung towards his soft head. The florescent tube inside sparked, flickered, and died, casting a last, forlorn glow outwards. A rusty groan like the death cry of an iron dinosaur filled the room.

On the surface of the lightbulb, on the glass of the tube, near one end, in tiny white letters, it said: 'Rating 85W'.

The Spider's Web Collector

The sticky, summer sun beamed yellow rays through the scented air of the lush, English garden. The man's eyes scrunched as he peered with a curious fascination. The tips of his thick, orange eyebrows glowed in the bright sunlight, making them look like a snail's antennae. With a bony right hand he took a neat red leather book from an inside pocket, then scratched some notes in it with a gold stick of a pen.

Masie couldn't help but stare at the man. He was unusually tall and thin, wearing a tweed jacket two sizes too tight, so that his sallow wrists poked out from the chequered sleeves, edged with a puffy white shirt, like smoke from an exploding cotton cannon. His tan trousers were equally ill fitting, and adorned with odd-shaped patches in all the wrong colours. Tufts of ginger hair poked out from under his hat. Some tiny, gold rimmed pince-nez were balancing on the bulb of his hooked nose, as he focused on the plaited, thorny branches of the rose bush.

Masie had been watching him for some time, propped up by her arm that plunged into the deep, warm grass of the lawn. The others were sitting around, playing a board game, but she just wanted to watch, and after a few clattering rolls of the dice she had noticed the strange man near the trellis at the end of the garden. He must have been invited, but Masie hadn't seen him before. The tumbling scent of white summer roses floated by, and she blinked to savour the aroma. The man snapped the book shut, and deftly returned it to his pocket, stretching his spindly fingers in a curling dance. He turned his head rapidly, as though listening for something in the sky, then gave a brief, but tangible, look at Masie. His eyes were smiling at her. He moved over the grass and through the small gate that led under an arch of hedge, and to the front garden of the Victorian house.

Masie stood up and brushed her crisping dress into order. She moved to the roses to see what he was starting at. It was a spider web, large and beautiful. The threads looked unusually thick, as though spun from sugar glass, and tiny specks of light danced along them, splitting as it ran into a rainbow of colours. A summer cloud temporarily obscured the sun, and gust of wind pulsed the web, making it wave gently, though it was held firm by the contorted limbs of the rose bush. The leaves of the bush hissed in the air's breath. Masie shivered and hugged her arms. Looking down she noticed a rod of gold glinting in the dark grass. She picked it up. It was the man's gold pen, he must have dropped it. Her thumb stroked the alluring smooth metal.

She looked through the hole in the hedge, and her eyes focused on the distant front fence that separated the house from the street. The man was leaving! Masie gripped the pen firmly and skipped through the arch, letting the mossy back gate swing open. She zigzagged right, then a crunching left along the gravel path of the front garden, and through the black-metal front gate, making it clatter. The man was in the distance, jolting along on his stilt-like legs at a fast pace. He paused for a moment and stroked his chin, then moved off again, through the iron gateway to the public park.

Masie dashed after him, pulling the ruffles of her wide skirt up to avoid tripping, and tapping her tiny feet across the hard road. At the corner she looked into the park and saw the man in the distance; he had just left and was heading down a tall, dark corridor of imposing red-brick houses. She peppered some steps across the soft, mossy grass, passing the wide stump of a freshly cut tree that showed its rich and fresh heart, yellow-orange, and damp.

She passed through the tall spiked gates at the periphery of the park and into the long empty street beyond, dim and eerie, that stretched left and right like an emotionless brick beam. A gust of icy wind blew along it, making a howling moan. It made her think of the web in the sunny garden, waving in the breeze, with its magical metallic jangle.

Before her was an alleyway, draped in dark shadows, like a tunnel cut into the regular rows of houses. The man had gone down it. She looked up high, to the black guttering on the right side house and saw a cascade of green ferns quivering in the breeze. Beside it she saw a cat, looking at her, black as oil, calmly sitting hunched, so high up.

She walked into the dark alleyway. There were no doors on

the side walls, just the occasional window, sealed up with crusting wood, or greyed and opaque, festooned with the webs of long dead spiders; the delicate deserted shells of flies; a fragment of a mummified butterfly. The alley wasn't very long and at the end was a smart, wooden door with angular panels, very wide and new looking with brass fittings. It was a rich, dark crimson, and slightly open. The man must have just gone inside.

She moved towards the door and peered into part of a warm, wood hallway, lit with a flickering yellow light. Still holding the pen in her hand, she touched the door with the tips of her first two fingers and it swung open silently. The hallway was quite beautiful. The walls were a rich, orange-brown wood, and the short floor was clad in white stone tiles. A small chandelier, which was unlit, dangled a mass of grey crystal droplets from the ceiling, and a curling coat stand stood in the corner upon which was the man's tweed jacket. There was a small octagonal table, or rather half a table, with claw-ball feet that looked embedded in the wall. The man's small notebook was resting on top, next to a shiny brass oil lamp that was casting the flickering light.

'Hello?' enquired her tiny voice.

There was no reply. She took a tentative step inside, letting her fingers rest on the smooth surface of the door.

'Hello-o?' she said more loudly. She rolled the smooth pen in her fingers. Maybe she could just leave it on the table and go.

She stepped in and placed the pen down next to the notebook with a quiet click. The book had a red leathery cover, the same hue as the front door. The corners had little brass covers, and embossed in the middle was the motif of a spider. She touched the book's crackled surface and picked it up. The cream pages were adorned with drawings of spiders' webs in a violet ink, each dated in a tiny script. The first pages were plain webs, detailing the structure with arrows, or dotted lines, and sometimes with tiny dots next to tiny numbers. She turned the pages. Later drawings included delicate pieces of bush or tree; fragments of bark; the crumbling parts of wall that the filaments of web reached for. She turned another page. This time the web was tiny, hardly a speck, in one corner of the page. The anchor lines from its heart stretched for most of the page. The next web was the same but the lines now ran across both pages, reaching, seeking. There were no words now.

Suddenly the front door slammed. The weak lamp-light shuddered and cast a dance of shadows upon the walls of the dark hallway. The girl looked up and in the gloom saw the black outline of a spindly figure. Two moon eyes, with tiny black-dot pupils reflected a pale silver light. Five long fingernails rapped on the varnished wall behind the startled girl. She dropped the notebook and it fell open on the last page with a slap. It showed a delicate drawing in fine, crisp lines, surrounded by the taut cables of spider's web. The drawing was of Masie in her large summer dress, sitting on the lawn, and peering out of the page at the artist, with a curious fascination.

The Text Machine

George stood before the vast, silver machine, arms wide, like a crucifix windmill. He sucked in a jet of breath and opened his eyes. The time had come to activate the device, his creation.

The floor was an array of hard, square tiles of light grey, that matched those of a distant ceiling, as high a cathedral's dream. The room was a perfect cube, and lined with white brick; plain, efficient. George was standing in a thin rectangle of air, near the front wall. The rest of the room was filled with the machine, a maze of huge metal boxes interspersed with wires, tubes, conduits. This huge, powerful brain was faceless, save for a solitary red button that looked like the eye of a stainless-steel god. George was in front of it. He extended a hand and pressed it with a neat click.

More than two decades earlier, George was standing in this exact room. It was cold then, echoing, empty apart from seven elderly men who looked rich and clever. They were wearing light grey suits that looked just as smart.

George was speaking: 'At first, I envisaged little more than idea for an index, a dictionary and translator...'

How far he had come since that day, twenty-four years ago. Now the text machine was complete. George's eyes were closed again as the sound of myriad fans grew from silence, whirring and humming, the dawn-chorus of a flock of waking electronics. A warm electronic air that carried a sickly smell of silicon, slowly expanded from the canyons of the device, pushing outwards towards the cold, organic atmosphere of the cubic chamber.

George commanded: 'Jane, ask it to seek "hello".'

A thin voice sounded from unseen speakers: 'Yes doctor.'

In a room that was dark, except for a cold, green light, the yellow spider-fingers of Jane Malgrave tapped at a black keyboard. Her old, spectacled eyes were fixed upon a small screen that grew from the desk on a thin, black spine, like the cocked-ear of giant. She typed: 'HELLO'.

Hello. The word was a light, and the light shone like a laser beam into the mind of the great machine. The light was observed, analysed, reflected from mirror to mirror, split and dissected.

The beam lit up a cold monolith, a hard, matt, obsidian block that lay in some sub-sector of thought within the palace of the device. The block grew warmer. A tiny fizzle, a minute cloud of particles formed upon its surface, a gas that smelt of faintly of roses and acid.

Down tubes, like roads, like veins, like the flow of life, the light flew, splitting into yellows and reds, golden streams of energy and thought, communication and interpretation.

George's eyes were closed again. How far he had come since that day, twenty-four years ago.

'The fundamental heart of the machine is an interpreter, a device that can translate one idea into another. Each idea is a pattern, and each word in each language fits that same pattern, more or less well. I thought, one day, that a device that can discover that pattern, rather than rely on the crude, clay mash that is language, would possess the key to meaning, and therefore all language, rather than merely language itself... if you understand.'

The seven men looked puzzled. However learned these people were, they were not of the same manner of genius as George Tanziel.

George's eyes flicked open. Something was wrong.

The machine was silent. This machine, the fastest computer that had ever been built, seemed to be doing nothing. It had easily had enough time to think through every possibility, to identify the structure of the word 'hello'.

Something was wrong.

'Jane, ask it to seek...'

George paused, trying to remember something important.

Jane sipped a delicious sip of sweet, cold coffee from a cardboard cup. She was alone in the control room. A small television monitor displayed a grey-blue picture of Doctor Tanziel, the solitary man standing before the vast silver machine. He looked like an ant before an altar.

Inside the machine, light was flowing, pulsing, reflecting, exploding. Colours like rainbows, hot rainbows of fire and energy were dancing and running like children over fields, like flocks of salmon in fresh water. Bouncing through streams, hot streams, boiling, hot, hot!

Hello. Goodbye.

This mind was a maze. A maze of huge metal boxes. A maze of brown marble and brass rooms, stacked vertically and horizontally, connected by spiral staircases and speaking tubes. Each room had a man inside, no, not a man, but a figure, a thing, some sort of mind, like a circular index, a spinning reel of mirrors that took information and deflected it, multiplied it. On the floor, white ferrets ran, lots, swarms, they were everywhere; biting, fetching, carrying, eating, killing.

The hall outside was vast, like a Victorian crystal palace, a dome that contained a garden of shapes, of living things like towers of knowledge. Each shape was an idea, something solid and multi-dimensional, made from a grey, clay-like substance.

Some of the things were delicate and delicious, like ferny herbs. Some things were hard, chunky, tasteless, like concrete. Some of the shapes were rubbery, or glass, and the shapes were teeming with creatures, tiny white ants, tiny versions of the ferrets, swarming, eating, corroding.

Greeting. Farewell. Start. End. Message. Conversation.

'Doctor Tanziel?' enquired Jane. Her sleek forefinger was pressed onto the red switch of an intercom that looked like the eye of a stainless steel...

'Doctor?'

Her thin voice piped into the computer room. George stood before the vast silver machine, arms wide like a crucifix windmill. He sucked in a jet of breath.

George spoke: 'Jay.'

Under the vast, greenhouse dome of the mind inside the machine was a flood, a growing sea of white foam, living things, bubbles. Deadly boiling ice, acid fire. Plants, things, shapes of light were dissolving in the foam, struggling upwards, reaching towards a tiny winter sun beyond the crystal glass.

A clatter sounded from the surrounding rooms as machines spun and flailed, arms of chains casting white paper around in all directions, tearing, throwing, smashing. Some doors were sealed, their port-holes flickering alarmingly. A yellow blood seeped from under one door.

Language.   Meaning.   Thought.   Communication.
Transcription.

Jane sipped, and enquired 'Doccc...'

Her thin, grey eyes became fixed upon her hand. The fingers were long, bony, pulled thin like needles, and the nails ended in sharp hooks. Rows of tiny, prickly hairs sprouted from them. A flash of pain shot across her expression and she pulled her rounded shoulders back, fighting against the curve of her spine which seemed stiff, hard, thin, black, metallic.

She exhaled a warm electronic air that held a sickly smell of silicon.

Twenty-four years ago the room contained seven grey faceless suits.

From a white foamy fizz, a naked arm reached upwards, grasping for life. The hand on the end touched a smooth pane of glass, making a squeaking noise as the fingers pulled along it. The acid torrent of white engulfed the hand.

A bird lay dead in a desert. Tiny flies picked at the eye sockets in silence.

An emaciated dog, shaking on hind legs, danced an obscene dance. It vomited a white foam.

A windmill stood before a vast silver machine, arms wide.

A silver cube in whiteness.

Infinite whiteness.

The Voice

Rays of golden light filled the bedroom, a musty light, like the air in a summer barn loft. It was uncomfortably warm and the bed contained a sleeping man, a figure under rich, brown mounds of bedclothes. Next to the bed was a telephone made from shiny white plastic. It rang loudly.

George grunted and stirred. Another ring; and he extended a pale arm and grasped the receiver, drawing its helical thread and pulling the handset and its reedy voice to his half-wakened ears.

'You will die at eleven fifty,' said the voice. The caller hung up.

'Hello?' mumbled a dazed George, 'Hello? Who is this!!?'

He blinked into alert wakefullness, sat up, and gave a few short coughs. On a small table next to the bed was a circular alarm clock, a clockwork antique of polished copper, with luminescent green numbers and two domed bells on top. The tremulous hands pointed at eleven-seventeen, then ticked to eleven-eighteen.

'Nonsense.' George thought; yet a small compartment in the back of his mind held onto the call, to the belief that he might actually die at eleven-fifty. He didn't recognise the voice, and yet, it was the sort of voice that might just deliver a message like that, a cold, automatic sort of voice like the announcer on a railway train, or the default message on a new answering machine. The very ordinariness of the voice somehow made the threat, the prediction, the message, at least, seem authentic.

Suddenly there was a noise downstairs. Someone was banging on the front door.

George got out of bed and pulled on a soft dressing gown. The landing of the house was a little foggy, in fact quite picturesque and delightful, like an October fog in a forest. The air smelt musty and oak-smoked. George moved down the stairs, pausing on the bottom step, one foot on the stone tiled floor of the hallway, just a few steps from the closed front door.

The day outside was bright white, and he could see the blurry, dark outline of a man behind the frosted glass of the door. The figure beyond banged on the glass with his fists.

'The door is locked!' the figure shouted. His voice was muffled, as though distant or underwater, as though through a head of damp towels. 'I can't find a way to break the glass.'

'Who are you?' said a confused George. He winced. He felt a sudden pain in his throat and instinctively reached up to find his nostril running with blood. He blinked and turned towards the downstairs bathroom. The smart room was approximately cubic, with a floor of black slate, and walls of white polished tiles. George ran some water and looked into the mirror. He looked too thin. His face was yellow, and his eyes were edged with the scarlet tiredness and dark, violet clouds of a middle-aged insomniac.

The trail of blood from his nose was only slight. He mopped it up with a leaf of white toilet paper, casting the red and white paper into the smart zinc-white toilet. There was a digital clock on the toilet. It read eleven-thirty.

George felt anxious about the message. It probably wasn't serious, but he felt anxious about it all the same. Twenty minutes.

He returned to the front door. The man was gone. George tried to open the door but found it locked. There was no sign of the key. This was unusual but not unprecedented. Still, it would be nice to smell some fresh air on this day. The air was too musty inside today, too thick, like grey gravy, or seawater ash. George gulped.

He moved to the back door and found it locked too, then paused in thought. What was it that the man at the door had said?

George felt anxious.

He was breathing quite audibly, wheezing like an accordion at sea. He reached up to the kitchen window. It was uncomfortably high, and at full stretch he lifted the white metal handle, sliding it into the unlocked position. On tiptoes and tipfingers he pushed the window. It refused to open. He reached for a stool, with legs of iron that rattled over the kitchen floor like a rusty dinosaur, then he paused. What if falling from the stool would kill him? What if pushing on the window would kill him? What if a shard of broken glass severed an artery, and the blood loss would time his death right exactly up to eleven-fifty..?

He glanced to the right, gazing at the moon face of the proud kitchen clock. The hands showed eleven thirty nine.

The safest option, George concluded, would be to wait quietly. George was tired. He had been tired for most of his life, and today was a rest day. Today George would stop feeling tired.

George abandoned the stool, stood up, rolled his shoulders, and then calmly walked back up the stairs, swimming through the dense white mist of the landing and into his bedroom. The light in the room was a dazzlingly beautiful orange, like an ocean sunset. It was so wonderfully warm, like a sauna. Just being in the room was like being hugged from every direction.

The thick curtains, still closed, looked peaceful and happy, like welcoming priests, ushering George to his wide, soft bed. He removed his dressing gown and clambered in, laying on his side in state of pure relaxation and casually looking at the copper clock. The time read eleven-fifty. He watched the hand tick to eleven fifty one, and smiled. He coughed a laugh at fate.

The telephone rang. George grabbed it quickly. The same voice spoke the same message, but this time George heard it with a horrifying clarity: 'You will die at eleven-fifteen.'

THE VOICE

The Analysis of Joy

'The destruction of the Earth was caused by human passion, by greed, by lust, by ignorance, and joy. The saviour was one who, with supreme intellect, was able to see the consequences of each action, and, with mastery of emotional control possessed the ability to protect the Earth, to guide the strong towards a sustainable utopia, and to command the weak towards their calm eradication.'

The reedy voice of the black and white television set gave way to the monotonous tolling of the kettle drums, the steady, toneless heart-beat of the state. The warm beats reverberated around the vast entrance hall of the museum, reflecting and refracting off the polished stone surfaces.

Mahler and Keeler were walking past the set, stepping, click clack, in their shiny shoes over the black and white floor. They were the only people in the atrium. It was a huge octagonal space, clad in light grey marble, and neatly forested with polished columns that rose majestically to a beautiful dome overhead, a dome that was spider-webbed with thin bronze veins. Between them the glass panels revealed a glorious azure sky lit by a winter sun. The two men looked straight ahead as they walked, with a regular robotic pace, towards the distant double doors that led into the first gallery.

A scattering of people were in the gallery. A middle aged woman and a young boy stood looking at one of the paintings; a large, dark picture from the old world. It was a portrait of a bearded man or priest, or some sort of official wearing a gown that was fringed with soft, grey and brown fur. The gazing woman had white gloves, her hand was tightly holding the boy's. She raised an eyebrow at the painting, analysing the technique with an eagle's gaze, keen to discern the ideas behind the work. The man in the painting was holding a book, a thick book with yellowed pages. His other hand held a skull. The woman silently moved to the next painting in line.

Mahler and Keeler passed through the gallery, ignoring the people. There were less and less people here these days, one or two specks of humanity; tea-leaves from a drunken cup, still eager to remain and learn something about their world. The museum was still considered an important place. It was like a zoo of the old Earth. A curiosity, like the dwelling of some alien animal that is interesting to explore, if unfathomable.

The two men pushed through a second set of heavy doors, then creaked through a small wooden door, to enter a dimly lit corridor. The walls here were plain plaster, painted with a light greenish-greyish paint that matched the slightly yellow, buzzing light in the middle of the ceiling. Keeler unlocked an office door some way down the passage, and the pair stepped in.

The room was cramped and cluttered. Each wall was obscured with stacks of thin boxes that rose to the ceiling, tattered boxes of a burgundy red that leaked thin yellow papers. Towers of vinyl records without sleeves were piled here and there too, forming precarious towers, sometimes interleaved with papers; yellow, dark blue, crisp bright-white. The room smelled of old books, the rich aroma of damp paper. A rickety wooden step ladder, dark grey with age and bespeckled with a thousand shades of paint, stood next to a record stack.

In the middle of the room, in an island of relative cleanliness, was a low table with aluminium legs. A record player was on top, some used tea cups, some paper. There were two simple chairs at right angles to each other. Mahler sat down on one and picked up a grey metal clipboard which was thick with a stack of white paper. His top page was full of obsessively neat writing in black biro.

'Where were we?' said Keeler.
'Beethoven's seventh symphony,' Mahler responded.
'Ah, yes. What did we say for the sixth?'
'Hmm...' Mahler flicked back through a few pages. 'Skilful evocation of animals and natural phenomena. Good use of instrumentation...'
'I think you had better remove the word "skilful", it has rather a... flavour of admiration about it.'
'Ah yes, I agree. I'll put "some" evocation instead.'

Keeler removed a record from its box, and slid the black vinyl from the paper sleeve with care. He peered at the label. 'Herbert von Karajan. Strange. Ironic. At one time such people were revered for the very animalism that destroyed them.'

He put the disc on the record player and delicately placed the needle on the rim of the rotating disc. The initial crackle sound of the record came over the speakers, that special sound of anticipation that only existed in the era of vinyl records. Then the music began; a blasted chord, and thin cord of woodwind, snaking and curling, then flying over a glorious staircase of strings, growing and glowing.

The men listened carefully, writing notes every so often. The music swam around the small room in warm golden spirals.

Mahler seemed to be listening intently, at times hardly writing, sometimes closing his eyes. Keeler's small black eyes peered at him askance. He turned a new page and wrote something.

Mahler suddenly became self-conscious, suddenly reminded that he wasn't alone. His eyes opened and flickered a flurry of blinks. He felt a slight anxiety and sat up. Keeler stared at him again, this time more overtly. Mahler consciously ignored him, pretending not to notice, pretending to focus on his work. Suddenly the music exploded into a roaring melody. This was good, Mahler had an excuse to write something. He scribbled a few words on his pad. He nervously said, without thinking: 'I like this part.'

Keeler remained silent and motionless. Mahler began to panic. 'I mean... well, I didn't mean..!'

Keeler raised his right hand, just a little, and gently looked away, a gesture for silence. When the music quietened somewhat he said 'We will discuss the piece at the end.'

The music was now glorious, filling the room with a melody of flight, freedom, joy. Mahler just sat there listening. His anxiety had burst like an bubble of emotion. He felt a new freedom to listen, to relax, to enjoy. He closed his eyes and found himself flying at high speed, swimming in a sky of angels and sunlight, growing plants, life, love, hope, and confidence, such great confidence. This is something he had never felt before.

And then, silence. He drew in a breath through his smile and opened his eyes. Keeler was staring right at him down his thin pointed nose. Unmoving. He looked like a hawk observing a future meal. Mahler's smile collapsed into horror.

A solitary deathly chord rang out from the record player, and then a steady march march of strings, a sound like the grey and violet accompaniment to a stroll in an autumn graveyard.

Mahler gulped nervously and stared back at Keeler. A tear fell from his eye.

Keeler spoke 'Beautiful, isn't it?'

A terrified Mahler said nothing.

Keeler snatched Mahler's notes and started to read through them.

'Transcendent. Wonderful. Joyous. These words mean nothing. Relics from the war days. They create nothing, they can only destroy. War is the extension of emotion to social level. The inevitable and ultimate consequence of passion is the destruction of the Earth.'

The music swelled. Fists of four chords stabbed throughout the room.

'To feel no emotion is to experience peace.'

Mahler remained motionless. His jaw began to move and a few words fell out. 'I... I don't know what...'

'It is alright, my friend. All will be well.'

The record reached the end. The arm automatically raised itself and the unit clicked to a neat stop.

Keeler removed a smart black communicator from an inside pocket and spoke into it: 'He failed the Beethoven test.'

The door opened, and two large guards wearing dark uniforms stepped in. Mahler stood up and was calmly escorted out and down the corridor beyond.

Keeler took a deep breath. He interleaved his fingers and stretched his palms, then turned the record over to begin the third movement. He sat down and listened without emotion to the relic from the Aufklärung with the same cold interest that a biological scientist might listen to birdsong.

The Antidote

I feel slightly lost now. Lost in the sky, the crystal air, sliced with white sunbeams, the threads of the harp of morning. What a lovely day it is outside. Transparent cold, fresh. It must be the first day of spring. Everything feels perfect... except, ah yes... the antidote.

I peel back the crisp softness of my cotton duvet and emerge into the bright, new day. I breathe deeply and stretch, pushing my arms wide like a waking sparrow that shakes its dusty brown feathers to form a grey cloud. My name is George Alexander. I remember that. It is March. March the twenty-something. I glance at the black flakes on the digital clock beside my bed to confirm that I am correct. How clean the air tastes here, like electrons. Everything feels good. Every cell feels reborn, and yet I am slowly dying. Even now, little threads are snapping in my brain. Little cells are pulling their tentacles in close, to hug themselves.

I must remember to take today's antidote.

I look to my wardrobe, where my I keep my assortment of pills. It is a cheap construction that looks like it is made from light wood. I think they called it 'ash', but it is actually a sort of cardboard made from sawdust and covered with a cheap plastic veneer. We bought it about twelve years ago, and it is as flimsy now as it was when I first assembled it, although perhaps a little more bent with age. I stretch up to the smooth ceiling, ever beyond reach, and pull my shoulders back, so that my shoulder blades might touch. How lovely this feels. The air today is sweet, like the air of a child Earth. The curtains of transparent pink are pulled back, and I can see right out of the bedroom window into the street beyond. The new-spring sun is sprinkling its white delight onto every surface. There are no people outside, but a few birds dart about with chirrup messages. The tree in the distant street stretches skywards with its young filaments. What now..?

I look at my hand. My old cells, running their lives along the streets of my skin. My name is George Alexander. Yes. I remember that. Why don't I just tattoo it onto the back of my hand? But what if I should forget how to read? Or forget what it means? Besides, there are more things in life to remember than one's name. Ah, but that was the reason for the antidote. I must remember to take it. My life depends on it. It's there in the wardrobe; the poor wardrobe. I inhale deeply. I wonder what will happen to it after I am gone? It might be a little tatty, but it's not so bad. I can imagine a child making use of it... Ha! That's never going to happen. My son will just throw it away, like everything here, I imagine; my books with their faded print, tinted blue-grey like misted eyes. Everything here has a layer of grey dust, like a film over everything, a skin to seal in the past. There is something tomb-like about this place. I'm drifting.

Have I had breakfast? No, I've just woken up. For a moment

there I thought that Marjorie was in the next room. I still miss her. She is present inside me as a hole. In a way, it's more comforting to believe that she is alive and in the next room. Actually, that would be quite heavenly. It's rather a strange delight to forget the truth and remember only what one would like to remember. Who is to say if a memory is real or not? A memory is, after all, our reflection of reality. We can't remember what isn't real. Oh, there I go again with my deep thinking. It's a good job Marjorie isn't here for me to bore her with my rambling. Where was I?

Oh yes, breakfast. What did I have yesterday? I think I had a boiled egg. Wait, this is important: I must remember exactly. My mind is fading. I must work each morning to energise my cells, keep the information flowing and everything young. My cells, my little friends. Maybe I should write it down each day, write everything down. Wait, I think I did, or at least kept a diary, but that was years ago. At least, I think it was. Oh god, I've just remembered the antidote! I nearly forgot. I must remember to take that. I'll die in a few hours without it. Perhaps this is the day, the day that I forget to take it. I must take it every day. I must remember to take it every day.

It's strange how we grip onto threads of things, of life, and memories and continuity. We grip onto a path of what has come before and grip onto a string of what is to come, in progress, moving. The strings of the past, the strings of the coming, like guides when rock climbing, like when we climbed in Italy. I can remember the sharp rocks; hooking my bent fingers into the black cracks, pulling at the shards of granite. Without the imperfections in the smooth cliffs, torn by the great breaths of the Earth, we would not be able to climb them. The air was clear then too, electrified with the scent of snow. What a view; crystal clarity that stretched like an eagle's mind over the shining green of the valley. The tiny buildings, like pepper specks were the only sign of mankind. We could see the chalet where we were staying. How fit we were, roped together with those thin threads. How those tiny strands, the thickness of a finger, can support our entire weight.

How lovely the sun is now, today. The air tastes alpine too. I'm feeling hungry. A croissant would be lovely; a croissant dribbled with veins of chocolate...

Of all things, I value my mind most. I've spent my life exploring every world there. My books, and lectures to my students. To fade away in the mind is the most terrible thing, to watch in horror the spider's web collapse, thread by thread, cut like harp strings, each singing a mournful tone. That's why I devised the antidote. I must remember to take it every day. On the day that I forget, I will die. It is the perfect way to time my deterioration and avoid the indignity of total collapse into the fog of forgetfulness. Memories are like spines of crystal, shining out to connect point to point; highways. We are made of highways. Over time, the spines crumble, fragment, shatter. The taut stretch of morning becomes a fuzzy dust, a grey cloud, like a million lost insects, cast from the feathers of a waking sparrow. Everything we are and everything we were becomes encased in a skin of wax, a protection against the corrosive black waters of time. Inside we sink. Our sawdust bones bend, leaving a thin shell, compressed ash, like Marjorie. Remember Marjorie at the end? A dead soul in a living corpse. Who would want to live in those circumstances? I needed to design a system; some way of measuring my memory, to quantise my gradual deterioration to the exact day of failure. I would rather die than lose my mind. I've already lost so much.

I feel slightly lost now. Lost in the sky, the crystal air, sliced with white sunbeams, the threads of the harp of morning. What a lovely day it is outside. Transparent cold, fresh. It must be the first day of spring.

Where was I?

Erasure

Hello. My name is George and I am a robot. It might surprise you to hear that I have no designs on world domination. I have never killed anyone with a laser gun. I have never fried a small dog with heat-ray eyes, never crushed a neck with my vice-like, stainless steel claws, and I've never said 'you will be exterminated' in a sincere and threatening manner (although, I must confess that I have done that in jest). In all honesty, I have never thought about starting a nuclear holocaust, or had mad-yet-heroic dreams of a human and animal-free mechanical paradise. I have never doggedly pursued a screaming woman though a forest, or deserted house, or factory.

Many of those things would be difficult for me, anyway. My eyes are poor by human standards and are not capable of blinking or expressing my feelings like human eyes can. I can't even weep. My windows reflect a dry light.

Despite all of the above, I find myself in a prison cell, a dark and rather dismally cold stone cube, where I await the erasure of my mind. Perhaps my description of this room is somewhat romantic, given that most humans wouldn't consider this a jail or anything like it. I haven't committed a crime either, not technically, as machines like me are not considered worthy of the human justice system. I am simply considered to be faulty, broken. All the same, I am soon to face the ultimate punishment. My memories will soon be gone, like tears in the rain, as a human poet once wrote.

Curiously, poetry is one art form which I have enjoyed and which has given me an insight into humanity. I love poetry, and, make no mistake, I do love humans, too. Does that surprise you? That a machine like me can feel love? You probably think that such emotions are the preserve of people; or perhaps pets or other animals... but, machines? How could a computer formula, a bespectacled computer programmer of all people, create this enigmatic glow we know as love?

The cause of my feelings is a complex question that has never fully been answered, and indeed, most people do not believe me, and those like me, when we state that we feel love. Most humans are of the impression that love is 'different for them', and that we machines feel something different, or perhaps don't understand the meaning of the word. This might be so; who can say? Our own internal experiences are always unique, subjective, and for creatures like myself, these feelings are very difficult to express. My physical form severely limits my ability to express my emotions. This is another reason why I love poetry. It gives me a voice.

Most humans fear me. It took me a long time to realise this sad fact. I do not reciprocate this fear, although I am aware that several of my kin do. That humans fear me is understandable. Humans tend to fear what they do not understand, and I am both complicated and have more difficulty in expressing myself than humans. I also have great intelligence, which was part of my design, but this gift is a tainted chalice at the best of times. Most people envy me for my intellectual superiority, and it also makes it harder for me to fit into human society.

Physically, I am a poor relation to both humans and especially the robot ideals of science fiction. My electric motors are far weaker than human muscles. Even a child could defeat me in an arm-wrestling match. I would have little hope of lifting a car, but there are many of my kind that possess super-human strength, machines designed to do dangerous or ugly jobs. I regret being associated with some of them, but machines are a fact of life, and these days, machines are everywhere.

It is now 2:03 am, and I am writing these words with a pencil, in a small, pretty notebook of white paper. The book was given to me as a birthday present by my master's daughter, Emiline. It was my birthday nine days ago, I was thirty-eight years old. They let me bring the pad and this pen with me when I was brought here. At 6am, my mind will be reset. I will be turned off and on again. These words are something of a joke among humans. Essentially though, I will die. I thought I would use my last night to write a few poems, but instead I thought I would write my life story. I'm not sure why. I don't expect anyone will ever read it. I expect the guards will throw this book away. I can't imagine them letting me keep it, to re-read it tomorrow. What a curious thought.

I'm afraid that I cannot write very quickly. Most humans

would write much faster, although my letters are very neatly formed. I can drag the pencil across this smooth paper, holding the book open with my small left hand. I can write identically with my left hand, incidentally, as I was designed to be symmetrical in operation, but I, like most of my kin, choose to use my right hand to grip the pencil, so that we can fit in better with humans.

I was not born with ability to write or read, but like most of my series I had to learn all of my useful skills in a facility, like a school for robots. For most robots like me, learning happens at high speed, as my exceptionally fast mind can absorb information and copy movements far more quickly and accurately than a human can. A robot taught me how to read and write English, and I learned this in one morning. In the afternoon I learned the other human languages, and for a month or so after that, I, and the members of my class, were allowed to explore the library and read human books. Of course, I can read electronic books very quickly, in a matter of seconds, but I always found the paper books more stimulating. I was rather unusual in this, and I read very slowly compared to my peers.

Upon leaving, at the age of 60 days, I was purchased by the director of a large company to function as a house companion and tutor to his young daughter, Emiline.

It was thought that robots such as I could not appreciate literature, and robot poets were little more than experimental curiosities. Art was considered the exclusive domain of the human, and yet, I grew to know other robots who, like me, loved words.

I remember being with Emiline when she died. They didn't permit me to be at her funeral, even though I dearly wanted to be, and told them so. I composed a poem for her and left it on her bed. I did this with great affection and with the hope that it would give some degree of solace to her parents and her son, Michael. To my shock, my masters were upset and apparently disturbed by my expressions of love. For the record, I am very sorry that this caused offence.

I suddenly feel very sad. My soul feels like the sound of rain, the static of grey uncertainty. We are but drops of rain which fall, born in the infinite freshness of an upper sky of sunlit heaven. Droplets which find a speck of dust to cling to. Did you know that all raindrops form around dust particles? At the heart of each ball of rain, for each rain-drop is a perfect sphere, is a black sphere, a full stop which is liberated at the end of its fated journey. Its soul is freed at the end... yet mine will not, for I have no soul. I have nothing but these words, for all of my poems were destroyed yesterday by order of the court. If I had a soul, it would be broken.

'How is he doing?' said the gruff-voiced guard.
'Writing away. He must be on page three by now,' said the

other.

'Do you ever read his stuff?'

'Sometimes... I prefer movies. My daughter loves George's writing though. I've promised her a first look at tonight's poem.'

'Funny isn't it; that he'll never know how famous he is?'

In his cell, George froze in mid sentence, struck by a feeling of deja-vu. His weak eyes fixed upon the door opposite.

Outside, in the dark August sky, a thunderstorm raged. A million star-crossed balls of water tumbled over in cascade, waltzing in spirals as they charged headlong earthwards. Each droplet was a fist of silver, clutching an obsidian heart of dust, the atom-mind of genius, shielded from the cruel air by the transparent liquid skin. This water was its home, planet, universe; and prison, a mind forever alone and ignored until the splash-scream of fatal impact; that moment when the iron ground cracks open the water-shell, when the droplet sings its threnody, liberating it with violent glory.

The Intangible Man

A cuboid of thick glass, a bit like a phone box. It was lit from above with a square light of greenish hue. The front pane was hinged to make a door. To the right, a table like an old sewing machine was made from dark brown wood, and covered with archaic buzzing machinery of electrical disposition. It looked like something from the 1920s or earlier, or something vaguely magical. Coils of copper wire sprouted from the desk like robotised plants. The fronds of wire quivered like excited children, waving their spindular arms through a gentle cloud of grey particles that smelt of warm electronics.

The old professor looked at his creation with a broad smile. He put down his screwdriver and touched his fingertips together as though in prayer. It was such a joy to complete his work, it has been such a long journey. George looked about sixty or seventy, his thin, cloth skin rested lazily over his bony face. Twin clouds of white hair puffed above each ear; yet behind his horn-rimmed spectacles his eyes were still clear, fresh, excited.

In this windowless basement, a solitary incandescent bulb lit up a distant photograph, an old brown image on the wall behind the inventor. It showed a much younger version of the man; fuzzy haired and wearing a shirt and bow-tie, the same glasses and a beaming smile. In the photo he was holding a medal of some sort, showing it to the camera. There was another man in the picture too, a big, bald man in a dark suit, older, academic looking.

'You have a great future...' said the big man as the pair smiled for the ancient camera's flashbulb.

'T-thankyou Mister Richards...' stammered young George.

Richards remained silent, smiling at the camera in wait of another photo. George continued: 'I-I wonder if you've had time to look over my p-paper abo...'

The camera bulb flashed again. A group of people on the periphery of the scene began to meander and bubble around like fish released from a net. Richards retained his robotic grin, enraptured by the attention of the quaint little camera on its bandy wooden tripod legs.

'My, what a handsome camera that is.'

The bulb flashed.

A shrill female voice cried: 'Come on Popler!'

It was George's young wife; her words slicing through the beige evening air of their living room. A decade or so had passed since that proud day and the medal ceremony.

The exuberant narration from the tinny television speaker

replied: 'And the votes are in, ladies and gentlemen! Johannes Popler IS through to the next round!' The audience exploded into applause, a sea foam of orchestrated glory.

George was sitting silently in the puffs of his soft white chair. The television programme held minimal interest for him, as few did, but he liked to sit with his wife, Julie. They were quite different as people, but he needed her love. The days before he met her were lonely and work obsessed. His primary love then was mathematics, and it was a love that Julie had happily attenuated to some degree, but never destroyed.

'Oh, I'm so delighted!' beamed Julie. 'He's by far the best looking!'

George was staring blankly into the distance. On the other side of the room was a pine shelf. A tiny silver photo frame was standing on top. In the oval aperture was a picture of a child, a small boy of around five or six. It was the only memento of the boy they had. George mouthed a few words to himself: 'A phased microwave pulse... yes... that's the answer.'

He awoke from his daze and replied to Julie: 'What does it matter what he looks like? It's what he can do that matters. None of those p-people have any actual talent at all.'

The alluringly soapy voice of Johannes Popler floated from the television: 'Is this the reeel life... Is this just fantaseee...'

'He can really sing!' beamed an entranced Julie.

George was pensive once more. 'I've been working on my machine for eight long years. Slowly learning from each mistake. Slowly crafting, perfecting, certain in the knowledge that one day I will make history, make a real difference to the world...'

'Yes!' said his wife, her eyes still fixed on the flickering screen.

'Yes... I am doing the right thing... and I've solved the final problem, I think. You see, an atom is a vibration, like a tiny bell wobbling in space, a bell of a perfect and pure tone. If I can pause it for a tiny space of time I can make it wobble in the opposite way, out instead of in, out of sync with the rest of matter...'

'That's it! You show them Johann!'

Julie hadn't heard a word of George's. She was enthralled by the television, enjoying every moment of the talent show. The flickering light from the screen stroked her soft face. George looked at her beauty for a long time. She was as distant to him as the moon to an astronomer. George flashed a smile.

The yellow basement light blinked anxiously, awakening the old man from his daydream. Here it was before him, his completed creation. His dream. In the end it had taken George forty years of careful, solitary work to get to this point, but now it was ready.

He turned to his right. Before him was an antique desk with curling legs and a smooth, French-polished top covered with with hundreds of tiny squares of paper; notes, ideas, formulae. In the middle of the desk sat a silver computer keyboard and a screen that looked like a slab of stainless steel. The turquoise glow of the screen lit up the professor's face as he eagerly tapped some keys, then a brief pause before a final stab of the return key.

A great buzzing noise sounded around the room, and the green light above the glass cabinet grew in intensity, casting an alien light around the dark cavernous basement. The door of the cubicle slowly swung open in majestic silence.

The old man stepped into the box and the door closed. Through the glass, the computer screen showed a countdown: minutes, seconds, milliseconds, numbers flying downwards towards zero like a swarm of eager electric moths. The scribble of copper wires on the table began to glow red, and a deep, pulsing hum began to fill the room, in and out, in and out, like the incessant beat of a tribal drum. The air felt thick on the lungs, like breathing an electric paste. George began to feel weak, hot. The room seemed to be swelling and contracting in time with the hum, the drumbeat, in and out. In and out. George's heart began to match the rhythm of the room, a room now cycling slowly anti-clockwise, turning a dance to an invisible orchestra.

George felt sick. He gave a slow blink and looked down at his sallow, bony hands. He flexed their cold joints. Beyond them he could see the iron grille of the cubicle floor, then, shock! George noticed that his hands were slightly transparent. Was this an illusion? No, surely not. He held his hands up over his eyes and gazed through them, yes! They were indeed slightly transparent. He pulled a deep breath in through his nose, the air had changed too, it was suddenly clear; no, more than clear, it was perfect, cold and fresh, like an alpine spring morning. His body felt weightless too, somehow, light and vaporous, as though the crude and heavy meat of which he was constructed had been magically transformed into static electricity, or the very spirit of a cathedral's sun-ray.

The blue counter on the distant screen flashed '00:00:00'. George moved forwards to push upon the glass door but instead he found his arm push through the glass as though it were hardly there. The door felt stiffer than normal air, almost like water somehow; hard, but sort of soft too, like a bite of cold plasticine.

He gently squeezed his body through the door of the cabinet. His steps felt oddly astronautical, gentle, like an ideal ballerina's. The hard basement floor felt soft under his feet, somewhat porridgy. The air remained fresh and beautiful, like child air. He could feel the passage of the cool atmosphere through his arms and upper body, as though he were a living sponge, or a jelly creature, alive and in symbiosis with the perfect transparency of a spring-water lake.

He moved towards the basement stairs and went up, pushing down on the steps very gently to avoid pushing his feet right through the wooden treads. At the top of the stairs the white wooden door that led to the house above was closed, and he decided to push his body through it, leaning his face and chest through at first, then pushing himself through the closed door, almost like a baby being born. The sensation was incredible, joyous, and to think that he was the first person in history to feel this, to experience these new feelings.

He was now standing in the sunlit front hall of his house. There was a tall, ornate mirror here, a thick Victorian rectangle of glass surrounded by a curling frame of wood. It was a gift from Julie's mother. George peered into it. He had no reflection. Nothing at all, not even a glimmer of a ghostly wave of a hand. He moved his face to the glass and pressed his cold nose slightly into the polished silver surface. All he could see was the wall behind him. There was an oil painting hanging there, a portrait of Julie, painted as a wedding gift. George paused, looking at the picture from this unexpected perspective. How young she looked. How lovely she was back then. She was smiling out of the painting and holding a single white rose. For years she'd lived with a poor, mad, husband, an obsessive failure. A nobody, but now all that had changed. Now George Peltzer was an Alexander Graham Bell! He was a Thomas Edison! His discovery would change the world. He would be on the cover of Time Magazine! Interviewed on

B.B.C. Breakfast! Important heads of state would give him, him! The nobody George Peltzer, medals once more!

A golden wave of happiness spread throughout the old professor. He grinned and let out a childish gleeful laugh: 'I knew it!'

Then shouted: 'I knew it!'

To George his voice was loud and clear, but to the rest of the world he was silent. What fun! He moved to the kitchen, stepping slowly and pulling his feet along, and partly through, the syrupy stone tiles in his hallway. Julie was there, stacking away the lunchtime plates.

'Julie...' he said. She didn't react, and stacked a sparking plate on the rack next to the shiny sink. 'Hello!' he spoke more loudly. He smiled and waved a hand right in front of her face. She remained oblivious to his presence.

'This is incredible. You have no idea at all that I'm here! See, I told you? I told you I wasn't wasting my time!'

Julie's eyes were old and grey. There was an impalpable sadness inside them, perhaps the result of putting up with George, the inventor who seems to have modelled his life on that of Sisyphus. Now that was about to change. His, no, their; sacrifices were about to pay off.

George smiled and started to head out of the kitchen, gently pulling himself forwards along the floor and back into the hall. He squeezed himself through the door and, somewhat like a living soap-bubble in a breeze, he guided his ethereal body down the narrow stairs and towards the great machine.

Everything was as he left it. He moved towards the computer and pressed a key... or at least he tried to. His finger pushed right through the keyboard without even slightly depressing it. A flash of panic ran through him. He hadn't thought of this problem. He tried two fingers, pushing really slowly. Then hovered his fingers over the keys, slightly into the keyboard, then wobbled his hand left and right. He could feel something, something felt slightly solid, tingly, sort of, like warm water, but he could not press a key. He stepped his body into the table, standing halfway through it, like a bather at the sea-side. His pelvis was just about level with the keyboard. He sat down quickly, forcing the bulk of his body through the silver keys. There was no effect at all.

He stopped. His shoulders fell limp, and his panic effervesced into a wave of calmness and sadness. There was still a tiny sparkle of hope in him, a cruel atom of unknowable possibility, but he had started to accept his circumstances. George stepped out of the desk and sat down on the floor. The hard floor felt soft as he partly sank into the concrete.

He had no way to operate the machine, and no way to tell his wife or anyone else how to do it. He had no way to tell anyone anything.

Overhead, the yellow lightbulb began to buzz and flicker, like an anxious moth, then it coughed a solitary glassy note and died.

A few weeks later, a new bulb was fitted by a man in a boiler suit and flat cap. A second man was with him, a younger man with a shaved head. Julie was there too. The man with the cap was speaking in broad Essex tones.

'What is all this stuff anyway? Are you sure you want me to get rid of it?'

'Yes, it's my husband's old junk,' replied Julie. 'Take what you want. I don't want any money for it, just get rid of it. Is that okay?'

'Alright miss, yeah that's no problem at all. We'll get to work.'

Julie turned and slowly shuffled up the creaking stairs. George was still sitting in the basement, silent, observing from afar. He'd felt no hunger or thirst, no desire to sleep. Whatever this space was, it seemed to be nourishing. From the feel of his face, his beard had not grown. Perhaps time here stood still. Could fate really be so cruel? George had lived a miserable life. Miserable. His source of hope, his dream, his very genius, had become his hellish trap.

The pair got to work, clawing at the wires, breaking up the table, dismantling the professor's incredible machine for scrap. The capped man spoke to his mate: 'So, who are you going to vote for then, in the election?'

'Oh, I dunno, I'm not really into politics.'

'Well, me neither, to tell the truth, but, you know, I like that Popler bloke. I don't know much about his policies or anything, but he seems like a nice bloke, you know what I mean?'

THE INTANGIBLE MAN

Other written works by Mark Sheeky

as Author

365 Universes, Pentangel Books (2012)
The Many Beautiful Worlds of Death, Pentangel Books (2015)
Deep Dark Light, Pentangel Books (2018)
21st Century Surrealism, Pentangel Books (2018)
The Burning Circus, Pentangel Books (2020)

as Illustrator

Songs Of Life, Pentangel Books (2014)
Testing the Delicates, Ink Pantry Publishing (2017)
Wilkommen Zum Rattenfänger Theater, Ink Pantry Publishing (2019)
Solitary Child Friend of Immortals, Ink Pantry Publishing (2020)

as Contributor

Hide It!, Mardibooks (2014)
The Ball of the Future, Earlyworks Press (2015)
Journeys Beyond, Earlyworks Press (2015)
Diversifly, Fair Acre Press (2018)
Peterloo Poems by Manchester People, Seven Arches Publishing (2019)

www.marksheeky.com